THE LARK WHO HAD NO SONG

CAROLYN NYSTROM

The Lark Who Had No Song

ILLUSTRATIONS BY
LORI McELRATH-ESLICK

A LION PICTURE STORY

Oxford · Batavia · Sydney

Chad's world began in a hollow tree.
He could not see the sun,
but he felt its golden warmth
spread down through his mother's body
into his ivory shell.
He could not see the clouds
sailing in the breeze,
but he felt the brittle limbs
of the aging tree
groan and ache in the wind.
And he felt his mother tuck her wings
further down to keep him safe.

One day Chad shivered inside his shell.
He heard lightning crackle
and hiss above him.
He heard the wind and the tree
shriek in chorus.
He heard a roar of thunder echo
a splintered roar from within the tree.
Chad felt himself sail high,
high through the air:
soaring, sinking, wings tucked tight
inside his shell.

A soft plop ended his fall.
Chad felt cold, cold—
colder than he had ever felt—
and very, very sleepy.
Slower and slower beat his heart.

But God, who made wind and rain
and thunder and lightning,
loved the little bird
still hidden inside his shell.

Hours went by.
Then through foggy brain,
Chad felt himself move again:
the gentle cupping of a small hand,
a settling down into a soft tidy nest,
a rustle of departing feet.
Moments later, Chad felt a warm feathered body
shut out the cold and light.
And from the distance he could hear
the silver music of a lark.

Chad slept a long time.
Inside the egg, his body grew and grew.

Chad moved his beak from side to side,
trying to find a more comfortable spot.
His wings pressed
against the sides of the shell.
His head pushed harder and harder
against the top.
His feet tried to stretch,
but the shell held them close to his tummy.
Was his egg home getting smaller?
No, Chad was getting bigger.
And bigger!

One day when Chad tried to straighten his neck,
his beak scratched the inside of the shell.
He tried again.
A tiny hole opened all the way to the outside.
He wiggled a wing.
Crack! A piece of the shell fell off.
He stretched a foot hard against
the bottom of the shell.
Crunch! Crumble! Craaaaaack!
Surprised, Chad sat back on a tiny bit of shell
and stretched his neck.

Soon Chad's mouth joined
four other tiny mouths reaching skyward.
Mother Bird scurried back and forth
bringing seeds and bugs and spiders
and even juicy caterpillars.
Chad's brothers and sisters liked the seeds best.
But Chad liked bugs.
He didn't like seeds at all.

Chad and his family grew healthy and strong.
"Peep, peep, peep,"
said the other little birds
as they reached for the seeds.
But Chad's voice didn't say "Peep, peep."
Chad squawked a noisy "Chu-urp, chu-urp, chu-urp"
as he reached for a fuzzy caterpillar.

Before long the five little birds
had grown enough to leave the nest
for a short time.
Chad watched the others walk in measured steps
through the grass under the fence
as they looked for seeds.
But try as he might,
Chad's feet always moved in hops.

Chad felt proud of the way his family looked.
He liked their soft brown feathers,
the gold on their chests,
the black stripes at their throats.
He especially liked the way
they could crouch in the weeds,
so low that their little bodies
looked like dried tufts of grass.

But Chad lost every game of hide-and-seek.
He wondered why.

One day the parent birds
lined their family up for flying lessons.
"God made the earth where we walk
and the sky where we fly,
and God made us," Father Bird said.
"We meadowlarks praise God
as we sing and sail through the sky."
And he lifted from the fence post,
fluttered a moment or two in the soft air,
and floated high, high, high
toward a white cloud.
A moment later he landed back on the post.

"Your turn," he whistled to the others.
After a few tries, all the birds but Chad began to sail.
How beautiful they looked!
Chad wondered if they could feel the wind
as it slid through their feathers.
They flew a perfect circle,
then landed back on the fence rail
with a bristle of white tails
and a chorus of proud peeps.

"Next," said Father Bird,
and he looked at Chad, still glued to the fence.
Every inch of Chad wanted to cut the air with his beak,
to hear the wind swoosh past his face,
to feel the sky lift his wings.
But when he stepped off the rail,
he forgot to flap his wings at all.
Thud! Chad came up from the weeds below
with a mouthful of seeds and a frightened squawk.

Chad tried again.
This time he remembered to beat the air with his wings.
They jerked him right and left, up and down.
They carried him a short distance into the breeze.
But they would not sail.

Singing lessons were just as bad.
The young larks already whistled three-note trills,
but Chad's best efforts brought only a raspy *kar-rump*.
And the *kar-rump* was getting louder every day.

From earliest memory,
Chad had seen one or the other of his parents
glide to a fence post, open a beak and sing
as if a whole choir of birds hid inside the tiny throat.

How Chad wanted to say thank you to God with a song
like that!

How did they do it?
Was it the way they planted their feet on the post?
No, he tried that and it didn't work.
Was it the way they stuck out their yellow chests?
No, he tried that too.

Was it the way they tilted their heads high
with beaks raised toward heaven?
Chad tilted his head the same way.
He felt his throat open wide.
Surely this was the secret!
He opened his beak and pushed with all his might,
ready to hear his own beautiful song.

"Kar-rump! *Kar-rump!* KAR-RUMP!"

Chad was so embarrassed by the last loud *Kar-rump*
that he fluttered to a nearby tree to hide.

Suddenly, Chad's beak began to itch.
He tried to rub it against his wing feathers,
but it still itched.
He tried to scrape it against his foot,
but it itched even more.

Then Chad spotted the rough bark
of the tree trunk behind him.
He leaped over to the trunk
and stood sideways on the tree.
It was funny how well his feet
gripped the tree trunk.
Much better than a fence rail.

Chad closed his itchy beak tight
and plunged it into the tree bark.
Rat-tat, his strong beak squeaked
as it scraped through the wood.
Chad pulled his beak out
and discovered a juicy grub
hiding just under the bark.
He gulped it down and tried another spot.
Rat-tat, thunked his beak against the wood.
Rat-tat, rat-tat.
Chad's beak didn't itch any more,
but he kept finding more grubs.

Rat-tat,
Rat-tat,
Rat-tat-tat-tat.
Tat-tat-tatty-tatty-rat.

From far away,
the trilling song of the meadowlark family
trickled back to Chad.
Its notes soared as high as their wings
sailing through the clouds.
Chad stopped his drilling for a moment
and opened his beak to try once more
to join their song.
Then he stopped,
listened to the high clear notes,
each tumbling over the other.

For the first time Chad knew
that something was missing in the larks' song.
What the song needed was an added sound,
a different sound—
low notes, rhythm—
his own music.
Chad listened again,
caught the flow of the song,
closed his sturdy beak tight,
and turned back to the tree.

Ratty-tat-tat. Ratty-tat-tat-tat,
sang Chad's beak against the wood.
Ratty-ratty-ratty-tat.
Chad's music lifted all the way up to the larks,
joined their song
and made it whole.

And God,
who loved all the birds he had made,
smiled.

Text copyright © 1991 Carolyn Nystrom
Illustrations © 1991 Lori McElrath-Eslick

Published by
Lion Publishing plc
Sandy Lane West, Oxford, England
ISBN 0 7459 2347 X
Albatross Books Pty Ltd
PO Box 320, Sutherland, NSW 2232, Australia
ISBN 0 7324 0680 3

First edition 1991
First paperback edition 1993

A catalogue record for this book is available
from the British Library

Printed and bound in Singapore

Other picture storybooks in paperback from Lion Publishing